GOLDIE
and the Three Bears

by Diane Stanley

HarperCollinsPublishers

Goldie knew exactly what she liked—

and what she didn't.

This made things difficult for Goldie.
It was hard work finding the perfect hat,

a really comfortable sweater,

or shoes that didn't
pinch her toes.

But it was worth the effort,
because when Goldie loved something,
she loved it with all her heart.

Every day after school

Goldie ate her favorite snack,

then she read her favorite book,

and then she lay down on her
just-right,
soft-but-not-too-soft,
very, very cozy bed

and took a nap.

Her parents worried about her.

"Why don't you invite a friend over," said her dad.

"It'll be fun!" said her mom.

But it wasn't.

Jenny was too boring,

Penny was too rough,

Alicia was too snobby,

and Sylvia wouldn't come.

"Nobody's perfect," said her dad.

But Goldie didn't want somebody perfect.
She just wanted someone she could love
with all her heart.

One day Goldie got off the bus
at the wrong stop.
She looked around for someplace
she could call her mom.

At the end of a tree-lined lane,

not far from the bus stop,

she saw a cute little house.

Goldie rang the bell.

Nobody answered,

so she turned the knob.

The door wasn't locked.

Goldie peeked inside.

She saw three sandwiches
laid out on the kitchen table.
That's when Goldie noticed
that she was really, really hungry.

Goldie tasted
the first sandwich.
It was too sweet.

She tried the second one.
It was too bland.

But the *third* sandwich was a revelation.

She ate the whole thing.

Then Goldie peeked into the living room.

She saw a book on the coffee table. It was her favorite!

She didn't think anyone would mind

if she sat down for a couple of minutes to read it.

YIKES!

Once she found a comfortable chair,

she settled in for a good read.

When she had finished the book,
Goldie peeked into the next room.
It will not surprise you to learn
that she found three beds in there—

and that one was too soft,

one was too hard,

and one was just right.

Within seconds she was asleep and dreaming.

In her dream three bears came into the house.

Then she dreamed that they went into the living room.

Now the dream was getting really scary.

The bears came *right into the bedroom!*

That's when Goldie realized she wasn't dreaming—

and that the baby bear was *mad!*

She took a running leap.

She was in the air—

The minute Baby Bear hit the bed, Goldie went flying.

When Goldie landed, Baby Bear went flying.

Here was a surprise!

"Whee!" said Baby Bear.

"Whee!" said Goldie.

"Stop it," shouted the other bears.

"You'll break the bed."

The bears were very understanding about the
sandwiches and the chairs and everything.

They even invited Goldie to stay
and play with Baby Bear.

And so she did.

"So," said her mom
as they drove home that night,
"she's not too bossy?"
"Nope!" said Goldie.
"Not too boring?"
"Nope!" said Goldie.
"Not too snobby or silly or rough?"

"Nope!" said Goldie. "She's just right!"

And she meant it with all her heart.

For Peter,

with all my heart

Goldie and the Three Bears
Copyright © 2003 by Diane Stanley
Manufactured in China. All rights reserved.
www.harperchildrens.com

Library of Congress Cataloging-in-Publication Data
Stanley, Diane.
Goldie and the three bears / by Diane Stanley.
p.   cm.
Summary: In this story, loosely based on that of Goldilocks, Goldie,
who has yet to find a friend to "love with all her heart,"
makes an unplanned visit to the house of some bears.
ISBN 0-06-000008-2 — ISBN 0-06-000009-0 (lib. bdg.)
[1. Friendship—Fiction.   2. Bears—Fiction.]   I. Title.
PZ7.S7869 Gm   2003   2002023843
[E]—dc21   CIP
AC

Typography by Stephanie Bart-Horvath
2   3   4   5   6   7   8   9   10
❖
First Edition

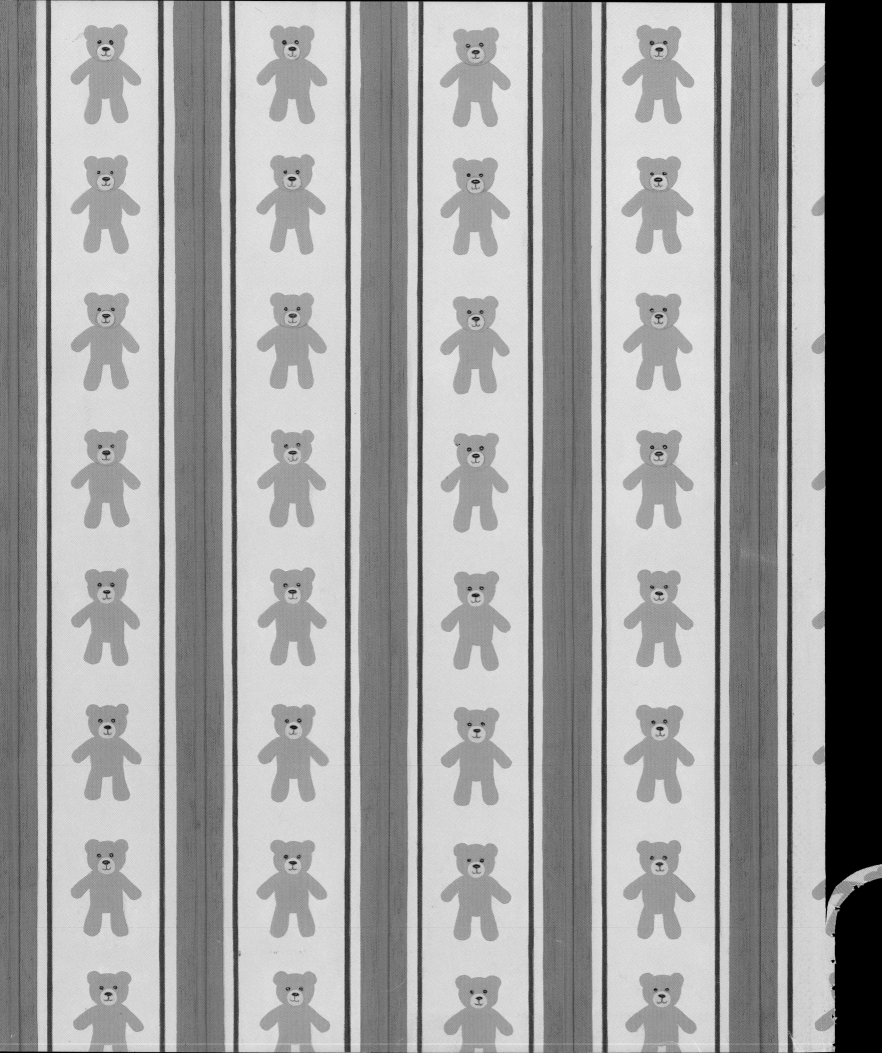